DO RIGH
and
FEAR NO C...

The Paul Gruninger Story

Eleanor Strauss Rosenast
Afterword by Ruth Roduner-Gruninger

Perfection Learning®

Cover Design and Layout: Tobi Cunningham
Inside Illustration: Greg Hargreaves

Dedication

To Enea and Noe Toldo—Paul Gruninger's great-grandchildren

To MayLynn, Kate, and Emily Dodge and Roman and Lucia Rosenast—my grandchildren

If you save the life of one person,
it is as if you saved the entire world.
~Jewish proverb

Do right and fear no one.
~Swiss proverb

"The Enea Luca Toldo and Noe Nicola Toldo Education Trust" has been established by the author to provide financial support for postsecondary educational opportunities for Paul Gruninger's great-grandchildren. All of the author's net proceeds from the sale of this book will be donated to the trust.

Table *of* Contents

Introduction

It was Saturday, June 15, 1996. It was a day that no one believed would ever happen.

Colorful flags decorated the square. Switzerland—red flags with white crosses. St. Gallen State—green flags with white bundles of sticks. And the city of St. Gallen—white flags with black bears. They all fluttered in the breeze.

A fountain bubbled with clear, cold water. As sunlight hit the spray, the water sparkled.

Red and white flowers were in full bloom. They circled the fountain. They seemed to sway to the music of the "Commander Gruninger March."

Ruth Gruninger spoke to the crowd. They had gathered to hear her. When she finished, they applauded loudly.

Then she walked stiffly from the stage. The mayor of St. Gallen helped her down the steps.

Ruth Gruninger looked beautiful.

Her blue eyes lit up a flushed face. Her smooth, short white hair looked like a cap on her head. Tears streamed down her wrinkled cheeks.

Ruth Gruninger walked over to the sign that read "Paul Gruninger Square." She traced the letters with her fingers. Putting her fingers to her lips, she gently kissed them.

"Today, my father is no longer a criminal," she said. "This beautiful square in the middle of St. Gallen has been named in his memory.

"It took 55 years and a hard fight to restore his honor. The Paul Gruninger Square will always be a sign of conscience and courage."

I read about this event in the newspaper. Just before World War II, Paul Gruninger was **commander** of the border patrol in St. Gallen, Switzerland. During that time, he saved the lives of over 3,000 Jewish people.

Mr. Gruninger's story caught my attention for two reasons. First, I am Jewish. I was living in America during World War II. But everyone in my family who lived in Europe died during World War II. If they could have been helped by someone like Paul Gruninger, maybe my aunts, uncles, and cousins would be alive today.

Secondly, my husband was born in Switzerland. He grew up in the city of St. Gallen. I am also a citizen of Switzerland through marriage. So, I am a Swiss American.

When a Swiss man marries an American woman, she becomes a Swiss citizen. She still remains an American citizen.

I treasure my Swiss citizenship and **passport**. I often think of what having a Swiss passport would have meant to members of my family who were trapped in Germany.

Switzerland

Switzerland is a tiny country in the center of Europe. It hugs up against Austria, France, Italy, and Germany. It is surrounded by very high mountains, the Alps.

The Alps separate Switzerland from other countries. They protect the tiny country from enemies. This is one of the reasons Switzerland is a **neutral** country.

As a neutral country, Switzerland does not take sides or fight in wars. The Swiss will only fight if they are attacked by another country.

During World War I and World War II, Switzerland was able to stay neutral. Many families from nearby warring countries tried to enter Switzerland for safety.

During World War II, Swiss borders were heavily protected. Patrol stations were set up. In order to cross the border into Switzerland, people had to present a passport and a **visa** to the Swiss border patrol.

Germany, The Nazis, and Adolf Hitler

Hitler became leader of Germany in 1934. The Nazis were Hitler's followers. They believed they were the master race. They thought they were **superior** to all other people.

The Nazis especially hated Jews. Their ideas were spread to the German people through movies, radio, newspapers, and teachers in schools.

The Nazis ordered the German people not to buy in Jewish-owned shops. These shop windows were painted with the **Star of David**. Signs were put up that said "Don't buy from Jews."

Soon all Jewish government workers were fired. Jewish teachers also lost their jobs.

All books that the Nazis thought should not be read were taken from libraries and bookstores. They were publicly burned.

In 1935, the German government passed a law banning Jews from voting. They were not allowed in any public places.

Jews could only shop in Jewish-owned stores. Jewish doctors and dentists could only treat Jews.

The situation kept getting worse. One night in 1938, Jewish businesses and temples were broken into, burned, and destroyed. Glass from broken windows was shattered all over the streets. Jewish people were beaten and killed. This night became known as the "Night of Broken Glass."

Jewish families made plans to escape from Germany. With their precious passports in hand, they went to Holland, France, and Belgium.

But soon Hitler and his armies overtook these countries. They brought with them the same laws against the Jews.

The Nazis quickly overran other countries. In 1938, they took over Austria. Then Italy, another country on the Swiss border, joined the Germans.

Switzerland was completely surrounded by enemies. But it remained neutral. Many Jewish people fled to Switzerland.

At first, the Swiss government allowed them to enter. The Jews were offered food and shelter.

But soon the Swiss government worried that there would not be enough food. They began to **ration** it.

Many foods were scarce. So people were given books of ration stamps to use when shopping for hard-to-get items. Before long, people had used up their ration stamps.

People found other foods to use instead. They used **chicory** for coffee and margarine for butter. Jam was made with so little sugar that it didn't taste sweet. Only small amounts of meat were used to make a gravy. Then it was spread over spaghetti or potatoes.

As the Germans took over more countries near Switzerland, the Swiss became fearful. They were now surrounded by countries at war.

Planes dropped bombs on the warring countries. Sometimes they missed their mark. The bombs would fall on Switzerland by mistake. Swiss were killed, and homes were destroyed. The Swiss people feared Hitler and his armies would try to enter their country.

In late 1938, the Swiss government passed a law to turn away Jews. Their passports were stamped with a "J." The Jews were stopped at the border and turned back to face certain death. It was at this time that Paul Gruninger, a commander with the Swiss border patrol, made his heroic choice to "do right and fear no one."

✧ ✧ ✧

Today, many people know the name Adolf Hitler. He brought a terrible darkness to the world during World War II.

Paul Gruninger was a man of special courage and kindness. He lived at the same time as Hitler. However, very few people know his name.

It troubled me that the story of Hitler's evil is so well-known. But hardly anyone knew Gruninger's story of goodness and courage.

This man's deeds should be known to everyone. Paul Gruninger proved that good can overcome evil.

After I read Gruninger's story in the newspaper, I wondered how I could get in touch with his daughter.

I asked a Swiss friend, Elisabeth Ammann, to find out what she could. Elisabeth learned Ruth Roduner-Gruninger's address.

I wrote a letter to Ruth telling her how much I admired her father. Luckily, she could read and write English.

Ruth and I became **pen pals**. We exchanged letters and pictures of our families. At this time, she was in her 70s and I was in my 60s. Here we were, two older women becoming friends through the mail.

I visited Switzerland often. So on my next trip, I made plans to visit Ruth.

We had an interesting time. We talked about her father and family. She told me what it was like to grow up in St. Gallen. Ruth shared stories of many of her adventures.

Ruth related the details of her father's heroic deeds.

And she talked about the hardships her family suffered because of what he did.

The more I learned about Paul Gruninger, the more I admired him. His brave efforts to rescue people he didn't even know amazed me.

Gruninger and his family paid a terrible price for his kindness. Yet, he remained true to his conscience. I wanted everyone—especially children—to know this man's story.

Today, not just adults have to make hard choices. Children must make important decisions all the time. Should they join in teasing the boy or girl whom everyone else is teasing? Should they invite the unpopular child to their birthday parties?

Many feel troubled by having to make decisions in these situations. They can choose to follow their consciences or go along with the crowd.

As a teacher, I saw children faced with these decisions many times. They need good examples and role models to help them make decisions. So I decided it was important to tell Paul Gruninger's story.

SWITZERLAND
1938

France

Germany

St. Gallen •

Austria

Swiss Alps

• Lausanne

Italy

Chapter 1

The year was 1938. Ruth Gruninger was away at school in the Swiss city of Lausanne. Her mother, father, and sister, Sonia, lived in St. Gallen. It was a three-hour train ride from Lausanne.

Ruth lived with a friend of the family. She was studying French and office skills at school.

The frightening rumbles of war had started. German armies had marched into Austria. Students from Germany, Austria, and France were leaving school to return home.

Every morning, Ruth looked around the classroom. Two or three more chairs were empty. The remaining students moved their seats closer together.

One Sunday, it was Ruth's best friend's fourteenth birthday. Ruth gave Trudi flowers and invited her to the Cafe Bel Air for hot chocolate and cream cake.

The girls wore their prettiest dresses. Ruth envied Trudi's grown-up glasses. They made her look very smart.

Arms about each other's shoulders, the two girls walked through the old town to the cafe. They kept their eyes open for good-looking boys who might wander by. The girls chattered about clothes, school, and their families.

Finally, they arrived at the cafe. When they entered the warm cafe, Trudi's glasses fogged up. She couldn't see a thing.

Ruth teased her and offered to lead her to a table. Trudi shook her golden curls at Ruth and collapsed in a fit of giggling.

Several days after the birthday celebration, Trudi received a letter from her parents. They asked her to leave school and return home to Austria.

Trudi's mother and father were worried. They wanted the family together.

Sadly, the close friends said a heavy-hearted good-bye. They agreed to meet again when the world was more peaceful.

One week later, Ruth received a letter from her mother. In it, she asked Ruth to return home.

Ruth understood why Trudi had to leave. But why must she return to St. Gallen? Switzerland was not at war.

Chapter 2

The train raced along the tracks
carrying Ruth home. The sound of the
wheels seemed to moan, "So sad, so
sad, so sad."

Deep fog covered the passing towns. Lonely, bare trees swayed in the wind.

In every direction Ruth looked, small mountains stood tall. They were like bodyguards in front of the huge Swiss Alps. She watched the landscape whiz by.

A knot sat in the pit of her stomach. She was frightened.

Ruth pulled her mother's letter from her purse. She read the frightening words again. "Dear Ruthli, . . . no longer have money for your schooling . . . Father has problems at work."

What had happened? Ruth was worried. She thought back to happier times.

Ruth loved her kind, gentle father. Even at 14, she still liked to hold his large hand and snuggle up against him. He would hug her and speak softly in his calm voice.

Paul Gruninger was a tall man,

strong and straight. He was gentle, easy in his ways, and quick to laugh. His green eyes twinkled through glasses perched on top of his nose.

In French, such glasses are called *pince-nez* because they pinch the nose. They don't have bows that hook over the ears.

Neighborhood children liked to be around Commander Gruninger. They would often wait near the garden gate for him to return from work. When he walked down the street, they would run to him, shouting greetings, "*Grüetzi, Grüetzi,* Commander Gruninger."

Grüetzi is the Swiss German word for "hello."

Commander Gruninger would lift up the smallest girl. He would place his tall hat with gold braid on her head. Then he would fix the strap that went under the chin.

The other children would squeal with excitement. They begged to have a turn. Everyone always got a chance to try on Commander Gruninger's officer's hat.

Paul Gruninger enjoyed singing. He was a member of the town choir. Ruth loved his beautiful tenor voice.

Now Ruth closed her eyes. She imagined her father at his beloved piano playing and singing his favorite song.

's Schwyzerlaendli isch nur chli,
Aber schoener choent's nit sy!
Gang id'Welt so why Du witt,
Schoen'-ri Laendli git's gar nit!

Paul Gruninger was commander of the border patrol in St. Gallen, Switzerland. His job was to make sure no one entered Switzerland without permission from the government.

English Translation of Song

Switzerland is so small,
   But prettier it can't be!
   Go see the world so far and wide,
   Prettier places you'll not find!

People who wanted to come to Switzerland had to present a passport and a visa.

The Gruninger family lived in a beautiful house in the center of the **ancient** city of St. Gallen. A large garden surrounded their home. Hedges of fragrant lilac bordered the well-kept lawn. Heavy branches of an old apple tree swished and creaked.

Nearby stood the **cathedral**. The bells rang once on the quarter hour, twice on the half hour, and three times on the three-quarter hour. Tolling church bells organized the day for everyone in the Gruninger family.

Suddenly, images of Lumpi crowded Ruth's mind as the train sped on.

On her sixth birthday, Ruth's parents had granted her a longtime wish. Ruth had received a small dog, a fox terrier. She had named him Lumpi.

Together, Ruth and Lumpi pranced through all the old streets of St. Gallen. They danced in and around the old church.

Then they continued down to the ancient town hall where they'd stop to get a drink of water at the *Brunnen*. This fountain bubbled with clear, cold water.

At the end of their adventure, Ruth and Lumpi would visit her *Grossmutter's* **kiosk**. It was located at the entrance to a busy train station.

Here, Ruth's grandmother sold lastminute items for travelers. Passengers could buy quick treats—

Grossmutter is the German word for "grandmother."

chocolates, fruit, crusty rolls, sodas, cigarettes, and even aspirin for headaches. They could pick up newspapers or magazines or buy lottery tickets.

Grandmother cheerfully gave

directions when asked. She even handed out train schedules.

Grandmother always had a treat for Ruth and Lumpi. After a big bear hug, she'd remove the silver wrapping from a round chocolate bar and break open a crusty roll. Then she'd place the chocolate inside the roll.

"*En guete*," Grandmother would chuckle as she handed the little sandwich to Ruth.

Ruth always tore off a big piece and gave it to Lumpi.

En guete is the Swiss German word for "good appetite."

"*En guete*, Lumpi," Ruth would say and finish the rest. The bread and chocolate tasted delicious together.

Ever since he had been a puppy, Lumpi had followed Ruth's father on Saturdays to watch his soccer team practice. Afterward, the players would stop at a restaurant for **bratwurst** and fried potatoes.

Lumpi would place himself under the round table saved for the team. He'd wait patiently for Commander Gruninger to give him bits of food.

One Saturday afternoon, Lumpi was nowhere to be found. Ruth and her mother searched the neighborhood. They could not find him anywhere.

When Father came home, Ruth cried out, "Lumpi is gone!"

Father thought for a moment. Then a smile spread over his face. "I think I know where Lumpi is," he said.

Hand in hand, Ruth and her father walked toward the restaurant. They entered the smoke-filled room.

A welcoming bark greeted them. Lumpi was sitting under the table waiting for his bratwurst and fried potatoes.

Ruth's father had not gone to practice as he usually did on Saturday. Some important business had kept him at work.

Chapter 3

Ruth's visions of home and thoughts of her father were interrupted. Sounds of the train whistle woke her from her daydreams. The train was approaching the station where she had to get off.

Excitedly, Ruth prepared to leave the train. She straightened her green jacket and tucked the white **embroidered** blouse into her blue skirt.

A loudspeaker announced the next stop—St. Gallen.

Ruth's sadness about leaving school was forgotten. Soon, she would see her family and her beloved Lumpi.

Ruth lifted her suitcase from the high shelf. She put on her hat and gloves. Mother insisted she wear these now that she was a young lady of 14. Then Ruth walked down the aisle to the exit.

The train lurched to a halt. The door sprang open.

Father called out his favorite greeting. "*Salut*, Ruthli." He grabbed Ruth's suitcase and extended a helping hand.

Father was not wearing the jacket

Salut is the Swiss German word for "hello."

with the double row of gold buttons. The tall hat with the gold braid and strap was not on his head. Ruth wondered why. But she said nothing.

Paul Gruninger looked older. His face seemed to sag. A sadness surrounded him.

Ruth hugged her father, mother, and little Sonia. "Where is Lumpi?" she asked. No one answered.

"We need to hurry home," Mother said nervously. "A snowstorm is coming."

The family trudged toward the bus. Everyone was silent.

The air in the bus felt cold and damp. Rain seeped down the windows. Leaf-filled roads could be seen beyond the swishing wipers.

The Gruningers had lived on Church Street since Ruth was born. When the bus stopped on that street, no one moved.

Puzzled, Ruth asked, "Shouldn't we get off?"

"We had to move," Mother explained tearfully. "I thought it would be better to tell you after you returned from school."

Ruth sat in shocked silence. Her heart ached. She stared straight ahead.

The family remained on the bus until the end of the line. Finally, they stood up and got off.

Ruth saw that they were in an unfamiliar part of town. Here, there were only *whonblocks*, apartment houses shaped like boxes. They stood gray and ugly.

The Gruningers entered one of the strange buildings. Many cooking odors greeted them. Smells of frying potatoes, sausage, and bitter boiling chicory filled the air.

On each landing, doors led to apartments where other families lived. From behind one, news blared from a radio. "*Achtung!* Remember to darken your windows

> *Achtung* is the German word for "attention."

tonight. Blackout shades must be used. Only the dim light of candles is permitted."

This was for safety. Officials feared that light from people's windows would direct airplanes to the town. Switzerland was not at war. But the fear of bombs was real. Swiss towns had been bombed by mistake several times. Buildings had been destroyed, and some people had been killed.

This **dismal** place did not feel like home to Ruth. Yet, it was where her family now lived.

The Gruningers climbed the stairs. Ruth's mood matched the gray color of the hallway.

"Which door is ours?" she asked angrily.

"Our apartment is on the third floor," Mother said in a quiet voice.

Reaching the landing, Father took the key from under the doormat. He unlocked the door and opened it. Ruth expected to hear Lumpi's welcoming bark. Instead, silence greeted her.

Pale winter light filtered through long rectangular windows. Ruth could make out a tiny kitchen, an even tinier dining room, and two small bedrooms. Only her mother's embroidered tablecloth helped Ruth know she was home.

"Lumpi died shortly after we moved," Mother explained sadly. "Perhaps the change was too much for him. He could no longer roam around the big house and play in the garden. Moving was a lot of work. We could not give him the attention he needed."

Ruth stifled a sob. Mother held her close and gently comforted her. "Sweetheart, Lumpi was already old."

Ruth's father seemed nervous. Ruth felt awkward around him. His green eyes were full of pain.

"What has happened to make us move out of our beautiful house and change the way our family lives?" she demanded.

With a trembling hand, Father

touched her shoulder gently. His voice broke. "Ruth, I *had* to help those families."

Questions tumbled out of Ruth's mouth. "What families? Why did they need *your* help? What did you do to help them?"

Chapter 4

Ruth and her father sat down close to each other. Then Father began his story.

You can't imagine the suffering a war causes. War is terrible, especially for children. They always suffer the most.

Many Jewish children from Austria and Germany have been sent away by their parents to escape the terror of the Nazis.

The German people have put the Nazi party in control of the country. The Nazis hate Jews and have turned most German people against them.

Jews have been robbed of their freedom. They cannot go to movies, restaurants, parks, or schools. They have been fired from their jobs. They are forced to wear yellow stars on their clothes. They are beaten, and police dogs **terrorize** them.

Jewish families are taken to work camps in railroad cattle cars. They are forced to do hard labor. When they become too weak or sick to work, they are put to death.

Ruth shuddered as she listened. She leaned on her father. A terrible fear gripped her.

With a lump in her throat, Ruth sobbed, "My friend at school—Trudi. She's Jewish. She just returned to Austria. Do you think she's safe?"

"I hope so, Ruth. Perhaps she is in Switzerland," Father said quietly. Then he continued his story.

During this time, many Jewish people came to our country seeking safety. For a while, all went smoothly. Jews could cross the border.

Then our government passed a law forbidding Jews to enter. After August 19, 1938, the passports of Jews were marked with a big red "J."

Jews were turned away at

the border. They were forced to return to Austria and Germany. There, they faced certain death.

People became desperate to enter Switzerland. They attempted to sneak across the border by crossing the narrow river at night. The lucky ones made it without showing their passports and visas at the border-patrol station.

"How could they do that?" Ruth asked in disbelief.

Commander Gruninger took his daughter's hand and tried to comfort her. "Do you remember visiting me at the station in Diepoldsau?"

"Yes, Papa. I remember. The border-patrol station was right at the edge of the narrow river. I especially remember the town bakery. You treated me to a special cake."

"How I wish we could return to that peaceful time, Ruthli," Father said sadly.

From my office window, I could see the river that divided Switzerland and Austria.

On the Austrian side of the river, there is a beautiful forest. In the springtime, new buds appear on the trees. In summer, colorful wildflowers carpet the fields. In autumn, the forest is colored with red, yellow, and gold leaves. And in winter, the trees are weighted down with snow. All is white and soundless.

I was commander of the station in Diepoldsau. It was my job to make sure no one entered Switzerland without permission.

Switzerland was an island of safety in a storm. Jewish people were desperate. So, they hired men who were familiar with the area near the border to lead them through the forest.

"Wasn't it dangerous? Who would do this?" Ruth questioned in a trembling voice.

Ruth's father paused and looked at Ruth. "For one, the baker in Diepoldsau. He was one of the guides."

Father sighed, looked away, and went on with the story.

Some guides were sympathetic to the **plight** of Jews. But many smuggled Jews into the country for what they could get in return. They helped the **refugees** find their way for money or for any piece of jewelry offered to them.

Jewish people were frantic to save their children. Suddenly, the impossible seemed possible.

The main highway was a few yards from where the refugees walked. Motorcycles raced by and flashed searchlights into the forest. Fleeing men, women, and children would have to drop to the ground. Sometimes, they crawled for hours on damp soil and leaves.

When they reached the river, they found it lit with ghostly stripes—the crisscrossing of searchlights. They waited for the moment when guards were not looking down from the watchtowers.

Then, the Jews quickly waded across the river. Many carried small children in their arms. Discovery by the border patrol meant all was lost.

One night, I watched a girl with golden hair wade through the river. She was about your age.

A border guard caught her.

Fear gripped the girl. "Please," she pleaded. "Please, don't make me go back. Have pity. I am all alone. My father is already in Switzerland. Please, let me stay."

She cried and tore at her hair. She threatened to hang herself.

Then the guard made a heartless remark. "It's not worth the rope. The Nazis will do it for you."

I watched from my window as she was forced to return. Despite her fear, she walked through the trees without looking back. Her frantic pleading pounded in my ears.

I had to make a choice. If I didn't save the girl, what would happen to her? If I did save her, what dangers would my family face?

Your mother had come to Diepoldsau to distribute clothing and toys to the Jewish refugees that day. When she finished, she came to the border-patrol station to say "hello."

I told her what had happened. "Help me, Alice," I begged. "Tell me what I should do."

"You must save her, Paul," she answered without hesitating. "Human life is sacred. You must imagine this is our Ruth. What would you want someone to do for her?"

Chapter 5

Ruth turned her sad eyes up to her father. "What did you do, Father?"

Ruth's father looked deeply into his daughter's eyes as he continued.

With lightning speed, I ran out of the border station and across the little bridge. The bridge connects Austria to Switzerland, death to life.

Mother yelled after me, "Do right and fear no one!"

The night air in the forest was cold and still. White flakes were falling out of the darkness. Moonlight showed footprints in the newly fallen snow.

Your mother's words echoed in my head as I followed the footprints. Soon I heard coughing and sobbing. The girl was lying on the ground next to a bare willow tree. She had tripped and fallen.

I helped her up. Gently, I tried to comfort her.

"Don't cry," I said. "You can stay in Switzerland. I will try to find your father."

The girl was scared at first. Then

she turned her eyes to me. "God has sent you to me. You are a man with a heart," she said in a grateful voice.

I took the girl's heavy **rucksack** and held her trembling icy hand in my own warm one. I led her back to the station.

Once there, I was stopped by the guards who patrolled the border. Herr Fehr and Herr Weder's faces were chalk-white, unfriendly, and forbidding. They were frightened and shocked at what I had done.

Herr is the German word for "mister."

"You are breaking the law," one of them said. "You will lose your job. Think of your family. You are putting your head in the lion's mouth!"

I paid no attention to them. Mother's courageous words gave me strength to make a tough decision. And it was the right decision.

47

I was commander of the border patrol. But I had to remain a human being.

That young girl was the first. During the rest of the year, I continued to help many Jewish people enter Switzerland. Again and again, I changed dates on entry visas to read before August 19, 1938.

For a while, things seemed to work smoothly. But soon, it was to come to an end.

One morning in the spring of 1939, I was enjoying my usual breakfast of coffee with hot milk and crusty bread and jam. When I finished, I dressed for work.

I put on my uniform, pulled the strap of the tall hat under my chin, and clipped on my glasses.

When I arrived at my office, a policeman was waiting out front. He pointed his gun at me and shouted. "Halt, Commander Gruninger. You are not permitted to enter."

I was stunned. I asked permission to gather some important papers from my desk. The policeman refused to let me enter. Someone had reported my actions to the government. I was to return home.

Several days later, Mother was busy in the kitchen. She glanced up from her cooking and saw a man at the garden gate. She walked down the path to meet him.

The man was an official from the government. He demanded the return of my beautiful uniform.

I had worn that uniform with pride. It was a symbol of my accomplishments. The power of that uniform saved the lives of many Jewish people.

But now, I was being punished by having that uniform taken away. My plan for helping the Jews would no longer be possible.

A quiet settled over Ruth. She clung to her father's arm. Her heart raced with fear as she wept. Her father put his face in his hands and sobbed too.

Chapter 6

The hard times began. Commander Gruninger was put on trial. The family could not afford a lawyer. So the state assigned one.

The lawyer was not sympathetic to Gruninger. And he did not present many facts at the trial.

It was rumored that Gruninger had helped the Jews in exchange for money. The court was not able to prove this charge because it was not true.

The judge insisted that Gruninger was mentally unstable. He forced Gruninger to have a **psychiatric** exam. This charge was also proven false.

In her heart, Ruth hoped for an **acquittal**. She could not believe that someone who saved the lives of over 3,000 people could be found guilty and punished.

The outcome was a huge disappointment for Ruth. The court declared Paul Gruninger a criminal! He was found guilty of breaking Swiss law, fined, and forced to pay the court fees.

Commander Gruninger was dismissed from his job. It was impossible for him to find another one. No one would hire him. People feared that if the Germans entered Switzerland, it would not be safe to employ someone who had helped the Jews.

Paul Gruninger was forced to sell umbrellas on street corners. Many considered him a bad person and troublemaker. Soccer teammates and choir members looked the other way when he walked through town. Relatives and old friends distanced themselves from the family. Only Grandmother was there to help.

Chapter 7

All merriment was gone from the Gruninger family. They continued to live in the cold, ugly apartment.

Christmas was sad and gray. Only little Sonia received a small gift. It was a sweater Mrs. Gruninger had knit. Unable to afford new wool, Mrs. Gruninger had unraveled an old sweater. She had made Sonia's new sweater from that wool.

Paul Gruninger's piano was sold. So were many other family treasures.

Ruth was unable to continue her studies in Lausanne. She struggled to find a job to support the family. No one would hire her because she was Paul Gruninger's daughter.

After many weeks of searching, a Swiss businessman offered her a job. His relatives had been saved by Commander Gruninger.

Ruth went to work in the office of a textile manufacturing company. She typed letters and kept the books. Her salary was 120 *francs* a month. The rent for the family's apartment was 100 *francs* a month.

A *franc* is a unit of money used in Switzerland. Today, one Swiss franc is worth about 60 cents in U.S. money.

Paul Gruninger earned only a little money from **peddling** and other jobs. At times, the Gruningers did not know how they would live from one day to the next. Their lives had changed forever.

Paul Gruninger was not a character in an adventure story. He knew it was dangerous to help the Jewish people.

Gruninger had been a commander of the border patrol. Yet this brave man had the courage to make the choice to remain a caring human being. This decision affected the rest of his life. He lived in poverty. He was considered a criminal. But his clear conscience helped him get through it all with dignity.

Just before he died, he said to Ruth, "I do not regret what I did. The refugees needed me. I would do it again if I had to."

Afterword

By Ruth Roduner-Gruninger

I know my father did the right thing. I am proud of him. And I'm proud of my mother who supported him. I am proud to have been part of this time in my parents' life.

I have worked for many years to have my father's honor restored.

In 1971, shortly before he died, he received the Medal of the Righteous Among Nations from Israel. This medal honors non-Jews who risked their lives to save Jewish people.

A **carob tree** was planted in his honor at Yad Vashem, in the Valley of the Righteous. Yad Vashem is Israel's official **Holocaust** Memorial. It is located in Jerusalem.

In 1993, Dr. Stefan Keller, a Swiss historian, wrote a book about my father. It is titled *Gruninger's Fall*.

In 1994, a forest of 500 trees was planted in Tiberias, Israel, in his memory.

In 1995, after 55 years and five previous appeals, the Swiss court granted an acquittal to the former commander of the border patrol who defied orders so he could save the Jews.

In 1996, the city of St. Gallen, Switzerland, named a square for Paul Gruninger.

In 1997, the city of Kiryat-Ono, Israel, named a public square for my father. The city is on the outskirts of Tel Aviv.

In 1997, a school in Vienna, Austria, was named for Paul Gruninger.

In 1998, the Paul Gruninger Foundation was established for young people whose countries are at war. It helps them seek safety in Switzerland. The foundation's goal is to get rid of racism through education.

I hope Paul Gruninger's story will inspire you to value all people and to follow your conscience.

Glossary

acquittal legal process that sets someone free

ancient being in existence for many years

bratwurst fresh veal sausage, usually fried

carob tree evergreen tree found along the shore of Mediterranean. It has red flowers and pods that have pulp that tastes like chocolate.

cathedral very large church that is headed by a bishop

chicory herb whose root is dried, ground, and used as an additive to or a substitute for coffee

commander main or head officer

dismal gloomy; depressing

embroidered   decorated with fancy needlework

Holocaust   mass killings of Europeans, especially Jews, by the Nazis during World War II

kiosk   small structure with one or more open sides that is used to sell merchandise or services

neutral   not taking sides or showing favoritism to one particular group

passport   formal document issued by an authorized official of a country to one of its citizens. It is necessary for exit from and reentry into the country. It allows the citizen to travel to a foreign country.

peddling	the selling of goods from place to place
pen pal	friend made and kept through writing letters
plight	unfortunate or difficult situation
psychiatric	having to do with one's mental state or sanity
ration	to limit the amount of low supplies
refugee	person who flees to a foreign country
rucksack	item similar to a backpack that is used to carry a person's belongings
Star of David	six-pointed star that is a symbol of the Jewish religion

superior	highest in rank, quality, and importance; excellent
terrorize	to fill with fright
visa	an addition to a passport by the proper authorities stating that it has been examined and that the bearer may continue traveling within a certain country

About the Author

Eleanor Strauss Rosenast is a retired teacher. She taught elementary school and at the university level, where she trained student teachers.

Ms. Rosenast is the co-author of two books for teachers, *Survival Kit for Substitutes* and *Do Something Different*. She enjoys cooking and has also authored a vegetarian soup cookbook, *Soup Alive*.

Along with teaching and writing, Ms. Rosenast paints. Her piece "Bearing Witness" was included in an exhibit at the Los Angeles Holocaust Museum.

Ms. Rosenast lives in Santa Cruz, California, with her husband Hans. She enjoys biking, hiking, swimming, and doing yoga. Eleanor continues to write and study painting. She has five grandchildren, who live in Seattle, Washington, and Redwood City, California.